An Autumn Tale of the Animals of Corlett Caves

An Autumn Tale of the Animals of Corlett Caves

For that which befalleth the sons of men befalleth beasts. Ecclesiastes 3:19a

written and illustrated
by
Sue Pumphrey

Acknowledgements
And Dedications

Cover by Bonnie Hill
Jewelry by Janie Pumphrey
Editing: Bonnie Hill, Dr Lisa Rasche,
Mary Howard Hollas, and Paula Fisher
Art Advice: Belle Jordan

In memory of Nancy Reese
who loved children, garden gnomes, and small animals.

Dedicated to Young People Everywhere

I've escaped into a gentler world.
Sue Pumphrey

Table of Contents

Chapter One: Lady Dill   1

Chapter Two: Lady Dill's Home   9

Chapter Three: Benjamin and Betsy   16

Chapter Four: Betsy Rushes Out   23

Chapter Five: Betsy and the Foundling   28

Chapter Six: Fielding and the Patchers   33

Chapter Seven: Ernest and Laney   40

Chapter Eight: Rob and Claire   49

Chapter Nine: Solutions for Lady Dill   57

Chapter Ten: New Beginnings   65

Chapter One: Lady Dill

Lady Dill hurries along the paths of a nearby wooded area of rolling hills, tall trees, and big boulders called Corlett Caves. Squirrels race back and forth with their youngsters chasing each other around thick tree trunks. Birds flitter about on their errands of hunting food. Deer wander through cautiously at dusk or before dawn because many homes for humans are nearby.

In the front and side yards of the humans' homes lay massive boulders, with many as tall as a meter. Between boulders, caves exist, and many different animals find the caves perfect spots to build homes. Other animals choose to dig holes at the base of tall trees or beneath holly bushes with a thicket, so homes can be safe from humans. Otters live closer to the creek in a valley below the hills, but one regularly visits Corlett Caves when needed, such as when someone's home floods. Rabbits dig their warrens deep in the ground with long tunnels, digging side rooms for storage or for rabbit kits to snuggle peacefully off to sleep. Chipmunks dart in and out of their holes, collecting tidbits to fill their cheeks to take home for their young to eat. Paths used by the animals criss-cross through the forested area. Lady Dill hurries along in case some younger animals stop to visit her soon for cake, cookies, seeds, or nuts.

Corlett Caves is a special place with animals that help one another. Some choose to raise young, and some choose to belong to a special group called Patchers, a group organized into helpful skill areas. The Patchers patch up problems. Thieves and scrounger animals also live in Corlett Caves. Scroungers don't ever want to work hard gathering, seeking, making, or hunting, and they never take time to make the repairs their homes need, but they slouch about, leaning on tree trunks, or hiding behind bushes or rocks, waiting for the busier animals to hurry past. A scrounger waits, ready to snatch up items not belonging to them, or as busier animals scurry past, scroungers call out for free handouts. One code of the forest is ignored by scroungers: *he who does not work does not eat.* A scrounger animal looks just like a hard-working, helpful animal, but the behavior of a scrounger sets it apart from its more industrious animal neighbors.

On this particular morning, a misty rain falls over Corlett Caves, and the autumn air is quite crisp. Leaves flitter their way down to the ground and sometimes swirl on their way down if the winds pick up. The paths and boulders are damp. Along one of the paths walks Lady Dill. She is an older animal, and her children grew up and moved away. Lady Dill's husband had been snatched up one day by a passing hawk, and though she misses him dearly, her friends politely respect her privacy, not prying into what happened to him, for the animal world accepts death and loss as a part of life in each animal family.

Lady Dill is a sturdy animal with a short, stubby tail. Some of her species have short fur, but hers has always been a bit fluffy, with white fur and two pale brown patches, one near her right eye and one on her right hip. Due to her fur being white, she often wears shawls of various colors, for white animals are more in danger out in the forests or fields.

Lady Dill is taller than the mice who scurry on their many tasks, and she doesn't have a long tail as mice do; she has a short tail that gets quite fluffy when it gets wet. She is bigger and wider than her mice friends. Perhaps she may be distantly related to Timmy Willy who lives in England out in the country. Lady Dill is quite fond of reading about Timmy Willy and his visit into the town, and she wonders if he is a distant relative, since her grandmother came from England.

On this day, Lady Dill goes out to search for food or roots, and she likes to look her best. Lady Dill loves to wear necklaces made for her by her daughter. Lady Dill polishes the stones on them until they sparkle, and the one she wears today is a pretty greenish blue.

On rainy days such as this one, she wears a thicker shawl, and today she wears a shawl in a pretty shade of French blue. To keep the shawl from sliding off her sloping shoulders, she uses a small clasp of a thin V-shaped piece of wood that she found long ago. She had smoothed out the wood of the clasp and glued a green jewel onto it. She makes her way along the paths on her back paws, but she can drop to all fours to rush along if necessary.

She is quite special to the community of Corlett Caves because she loves to learn about plants and roots that help the animals heal. Her real name is Dillweed, but she does not care for that name, preferring to be called Dill or Dilly. Out of love and respect for her helpfulness, the other animals call her Lady Dill.

Lady Dill scurries with a slow wobble along the dirt paths until two large, gray granite boulders rise in front of her. One flat, cracked boulder lies in front, but her home is in the back, in a cave between two boulders. Closer to the boulders she goes, carefully and rather slowly. She knows that if she scurries quickly, she might drop items. A steady pace seems perfect for her to get where she is going without dropping items. She doesn't like leaving her home too long, but of course gathering food and medicinal plants is essential to her.

Today she walks on her two back paws because she carries a burlap bag, for she's gathering roots, seeds, leaves, berries, and flowers she knows she may need to help her friends of Corlett Caves. Sometimes she passes an idle animal with an acorn lid held out, and today Lady Dill drops a berry or two into the acorn lid as she hurries toward her home. *It is important to help those who are less fortunate,* she thinks as she hurries home, but Lady Dill shakes her head, wondering if she is helping an animal who truly needs help or one who wants free food. *I dare say I am so confused about what I should do,* she thinks.

4

On this particular morning, Lady Dill stops and squeals soft sounds of happiness, for a small mound of carrot peelings sits in front of the two boulders. "How nice that lady human is! These will make such a delicious supper for me." Gathering up her treat, she sets the carrot peelings in the top of her burlap bag, and she makes her way between the two boulders towards her home. Shafts of sunlight shine downwards through cracks in her boulder home whenever the rain takes a break from drizzling down. The human lady watches the animals from her yard.

One day a few years back, a baby squirrel had fallen from its nest. Lady Dill watched the human lady hurry into her home, return outside a basket with a handle, put leaves in it, and carefully gather up the squirrel baby with large leaves, so as not to touch the baby with human scent. This basket with handles, the human lady hung on a low branch. Many an animal will reject its own young once human scent is upon the little one. The human lady hung the basket up on a low branch, and the next morning, the baby squirrel was back at home with the other baby squirrels. The mama squirrel was so delighted. The news of the rescued baby squirrel traveled quickly to the animals of Corlett Caves, and they trusted the lady human yet kept their distance.

This day, the boulders still hold onto last night's colder air, so Lady Dill pulls her shawl tighter around her neck. Down the well-worn path she walks along with the pads of her paws feeling the coolness of the softened earth. She hears nothing of the rain now, but she hears a low rumble of thunder sounds in the distance overhead. The rumbles of thunder continue as Lady Dill reaches her door.

Seeing her door ajar, she cries out her alarm, "Oh no! Not again!" She goes inside and looks about, seeing her home a complete mess. She looks for missing items. Pillows lie askew all around the room. Baskets of roots are overturned. Seeds still roll and tumble, loosely scattering on shelves and dropping to the floor. Clothing and shawls lay in a messy bundle. Small bowls lie on the floor with their contents spilling out near each bowl. Muddy paw prints smear in brown, criss-cross patterns all over her floors.

She clicks her teeth together in particular disgust at the invasion of her special home. Smoothing back her fur and the fur of her puffy tail until it is flat again, she begins to clean up the mess to restore her home to a calm place.

Meanwhile, outside in the crisp autumn afternoon, a small, gray mouse darts towards the road, the most dangerous place for any animal in the area of Corlett Caves. The mouse sees a vehicle coming, so he darts quickly back to the grass. Far to the right of the mouse, a gray-muzzled old beagle stands with a confused look on his face.

This beagle lives with a great many other beagles in someone's backyard, though he escapes from time to time when he sniffs a mouse darting past. The loud calls from the other beagles call out to him, urging him to continue his pursuit, but in the misty rainy weather, he no longer locates the scent. A beagle runs as long as it can after a scent, often getting lost from its home, so it is good that the old beagle stops to reconsider. He begins a mournful howl, "Woooooooh, I want to get back home before supper, but the other beagles will ask me about my prey." Knowing he's too old to keep running but not too old for supper, the beagle heads back to squeeze himself under the old fence, back with the other beagles, without catching any further sight or scent of the gray mouse.

The other beagles bark and howl at him, "You are giving beagles a bad name!"

"What? You climb back under the fence, giving up the search, to take a break in the yard? I'm shocked!"

"You must follow the scent!"

"Beagles everywhere are going to be quite dismayed."

One young beagle puppy starts barking about wanting a cheeseburger. The old beagle's eyes twinkle, as the puppy gives him an idea. The old dog feels tired with his joints stiffening in the damp weather. His tummy rumbles, and he wants his supper, so he ignores the calls of the other beagles.

"What's for supper?" he howls at them, knowing their younger minds will then turn to thoughts of warm food. The old beagle nods to himself upon seeing his younger companions romping about in eagerness for supper. None of the beagles notice the small gray mouse darting between the boulders towards Lady Dill's home.

Chapter Two: Lady Dill's Home

In the dim light, Lady Dill looks about at the mess all about her living area, but she hangs up her shawl on a wooden peg, and she picks up, sweeps up, mops up, fluffs up, gathers up, hurrying in setting chairs and little tables upright again. Lady Dill notices her grandmother's painting of mountains was taken down, rehung but knocked askew. She shakes her head, wondering why anyone would want to remove the painting then re-hang it askew. *Hmm,* she thinks, *perhaps a thief imagined that behind a painting is a hidden spot for valuables.* She carefully takes her painting in her paws, hanging it up straight before smoothing her green and blue plaid flannel quilt on her bed. Lady Dill takes careful notes of anything missing. She pulls a scrap of paper and a pencil from a drawer and begins making a note of what she cannot find. Soon a few items make up her list, leaving her wiping a tear or two, and she finishes tidying up. She put her name on the list in case she needs to hand it to someone.

Letting out a big sigh, she places her doormat outside her doorway, sweeping it off to be sure of a tidy look when guests come by, and then she carefully shuts her wooden front door that Rob, a carpenter rabbit, made for her. She never leaves her door open while on her morning walks. She looks at her tidy home and lets out a big sigh thinking, *I'm home.* She sets out her tea items and warms her carrot peelings for just a few minutes in a pot on her tiny stove. Lady Dill smiles a bit when she takes down a blue and white teacup from a shelf in her kitchen, turning it and admiring it as a loving gift from her English grandmother. A whistling tea kettle stops her daydreaming.

Her tiny pot whistles its shrill blast. Sprinkling some dried raspberry leaves into a cup, she soon pours steaming water into the cup. She sets her carrot peelings into a blue bowl. While the raspberry leaves soak and spread their flavor, she looks about her now-tidy room. She begins thinking that she'll need to see if anyone has a basket or two to sell, so she can put a few more things away and out of sight.

Three soft sofas make a cozy sitting place for her, her family, friends, and visitors. Each sofa comes apart with pegs which are useful for moving the sofas. She settles down on her blue sofa with her cup of tea and her bowl of carrots on the table beside her, wrapping her cold paws around the warmth of the cup, sniffing the aroma of raspberry tea wafting around her face. She wiggles about gently as she settles herself with pillows. She settles back, letting the tea's scent and taste envelope her. Lady Dill thinks about her home and how to improve things. *I'll need to ask the Patchers to keep a look-out in case any of my missing items turn up somewhere,* she thinks.

In the animal world of Corlett Caves, a Patcher is an adult animal, with some young adults and some older adults. Patchers want to be more active in doing helpful tasks. They could go by any other name, such as Helpers or Guides, but for some reason, Patchers seems to be the chosen name in Corlett Caves.

Lady Dill knows Patchers are young adult animals in a certain stage of their lives, working in many branches of helpful tasks for everything coming up in the animal community. Their forces of young adults can move quickly and are without their own little ones, and since the animal mothers and fathers and grandparents tend towards being busy, they are often too tired to have many errands quickly accomplished. Lady Dill hopes the Patchers find someone with keen observation skills to keep a sly and subtle lookout for her missing things.

Lady Dill, shifting herself a bit on the sofa, looks at the painting as it hangs in its proper place above her bed, remembering her grandfather and his travels. The blues and greens of the water at the base of the tall, green mountains stand out against the gray granite walls. Lady Dill sets down her teacup and her bowl of carrot peelings, and she reads a framed, stitched saying from her English grandmother, "Travel near or travel far, Home is Home, and Home is Best." Lady Dill pulls a purple shawl from the sofa and tosses one end of it into the air for it to land softly on her. As she grows warmer, she snuggles down on the sofa and soon dozes off.

Quite suddenly she hears a fervent squeaking of the most minute volume. "Excuse me! I'm so terribly sorry to bother you," a tiny voice went on to say, while the visitor knocks on the wooden door.

Lady Dill blinks her eyes open and scoots on her two back paws over to her front door, opening it to see a tiny gray mouse. "Oh, I don't think we've met," she squeaks cheerfully in as soft a squeak as she can manage, knowing he might be overwhelmed with a louder voice. "I am Dill or Dilly, or some call me Lady Dill." Mice live in abundant numbers and prefer to hide away for much of the time, keeping busy with so many little ones and so many activities. She asks him quietly for his name.

"Oh, my name is Benjamin, miss. I-I mean Lady Dill," Benjamin squeaks. Nervously he stands on the doormat, rubbing his front paws together, then flicking water from his fur off and into the space behind him. *What a thoughtful, little fellow I find him to be*, Lady Dill thinks. His gray fur, damp from the misty rain, drips and puddles below onto the doormat, but that seems a good place for a puddle to settle. On his slender back, he wears a dark green backpack. He trembles slightly as he explains his purpose, "My wife told me to see you, and on my way, that old beagle squeezed under his fence again, and he chased me. I bet he

caught my scent as I scurried across a covered patio where the ground is dry, but I lost him, I think, in the damp grass. My, it was the scare of my life being chased by a beagle! They don't tend to stop following a scent." Pausing a bit, he seems to be collecting his thoughts. "Lady Dill, thank you so much for helping us. I have a wife and little ones at home, and three or four of the babies have gotten a rash. We just feel a bit overwhelmed. Well, a lot overwhelmed..." His voice drifts off as he thinks over his words. "My wife says she knows you, and she feels you might have something that could help."

"Oh, yes, I believe I have something," she squeaks in the softest squeak while walking to her shelves on the sides of her bed, built as one big shelves-bed unit into the wall. Looking and sorting through bottles, jars, twigs, leaves, seeds, and roots, Lady Dill lines up items and puts other items carefully in drawers when possible, with a few mortar and pestle items and a few bowls set aside near rows of books on herbal cures. Seeds spilling out roll around on a shelf, so Lady Dill scoops against the spilled seeds with one paw, pushing those seeds to let them drop into a bowl. She carefully looks around at her bottles, choosing a tiny one, popping off its cork lid. "Could you hold this, please?" She hands Benjamin the empty bottle, setting the cork down nearby. "Hmmmm," she mutters quietly, thumbing through one of her books until finding the page she needs. "Oh, here we go, tea tree oil, quite good for little rashes." She bends down to pull out a tiny carved wooden funnel, and she pours a bit of the tea tree oil into the bottle and corks it shut. "Just tell your wife to use it sparingly, for this will go far with such tiny babies," Lady Dill squeaks in her kindest voice to Benjamin. "You say your wife knows me, and I do have a few mice friends, but I don't know which mouse is your wife." Lady Dill smiles.

"Oh, my wife is Betsy, and she speaks so highly of her dear friend, Lady Dill, so I am quite glad to meet you!" Benjamin smiles, looking at Lady Dill while clutching the tiny green bottle in his front paws.

"Betsy is such a lovely creature," Lady Dill squeaks to him, and considering how he hurried off to help his wife on this rainy afternoon in autumn, Lady Dill thinks, *he is quite wonderful for Betsy.* As they say their good-byes, Lady Dill squeaks, "I daresay you're both so busy with little ones, and how kind you are to her!" Lady Dill smiles, seeing him so quickly head towards his home. She pulls her door tightly shut. *Now I can put Betsy's husband to mind when next I see her,* she thinks as she goes back to her shelves to straighten up. Lady Dill smiles as she tidies her working area of medicinal items, imagining how it's so wonderful that Benjamin helps his family, so his wife doesn't have to venture out into the misty afternoon's autumn rain.

Chapter Three: Benjamin and Betsy

Benjamin scurries along the paths among the tall trees and boulders, clutching the bottle from Lady Dill carefully in his front paws. These narrow paths he uses twist through fallen twigs and around trees and bushes and serve as roads for the many mice. Benjamin keeps looking around in case the old beagle sniffs about nearby. He holds the bottle of tea tree oil in one paw against his chest as he makes his way on three paws under the twigs and vines that make the thicket. The rain drizzles occasionally onto him, so he stops, opens his backpack, and pulls out his newsboy cap to wear on his small head.

At the base of a tall red oak, Benjamin hurries down a hole and into his home. The hole turns a few times and has a few compartments for rainwater to collect and for storage of nuts and berries, but then his home opens up into a place with soft brown dirt walls. He hangs up his cap as he reaches the main room.

Setting down the bottle and gathering a leaf, he calls to his wife, "Betsy, I'm home! Lady Dill is so nice. She says this tea tree oil will help." As Betsy's arms are full of babies, he explains as he picks up the tea tree oil bottle, "We're to put one drop on a saucer, and then we can dab a bit on each of the babies' rash areas, using the tip of a leaf." He gets a broken saucer from a kitchen cabinet and carefully puts one drop on the saucer.

"Oh, how wonderful," says Betsy. Standing nearby, she holds three babies, and one curls up at her feet, and four others snuggle in a bed of pine straw. "I'll get started right away." She uses the pointed tip of a leaf to dip into the oil, and Benjamin helps her until each baby has a bit of tea tree oil on all rash spots. "Let's get these babies down for their naps now." Betsy snuggles each one, calling them by name softly as they snuggle into sleep, "Andrew, Brandie, Charlie, Dean, Edward, Fawn, Grayfur, and Hairy-Hazelnut, Mama loves you! Oh, dear, Benjamin, five boys and three girls do make for much work!"

"Pretty cool idea you had, using the alphabet to name this bunch," squeaks Benjamin.

As their babies snuggle together in the pine straw for a nap, Betsy and Benjamin gather loose acorn caps from around their home. Some acorn caps Benjamin wants for bowls. Betsy wants to save several single caps and use a double cap this day. She pulls coarse threads from a bit of burlap, and she fashions two little sacks of thick, green magnolia leaves to fasten them with thread onto the double acorn, making two packs. "It will take me some time, to later fasten each green sack onto the sides of the twin acorn pack." She begins without taking time to rest, for most mice always enjoy hard work. "Benjamin, when we go to gather berries, you'll be able to carry more once I have this two-sided backpack made."

"Yes, dear," Benjamin says absentmindedly. He feels so tired from his fast treks chased by a beagle through the forest to Lady Dill's and back. "I definitely will gather Lady Dill some berries as payment for her help as soon as I rest up a bit." Benjamin scratches his head and remembers, as he settles into an armchair to rest. "I sure am glad you like to make things, Betsy. A cousin of mine makes the nicest baby cradles out of pecan outer shells. Well, from the husks, I mean, the husks that fall to the ground when the squirrels are up in the trees, peeling back husks to find pecans inside," he tells Betsy. "My cousin uses a tiny chisel to make the beds just right," Benjamin says.

"Oh, my, what I could do with a few of those little beds." She knows her babies grow quickly and will soon be moving on to their own lives, but while they nestle in the pine straw, she daydreams of having baby beds to use, even though her babies will soon grow out of them.

18

She makes three tiny strips of twine using some thin grapevines gathered from outside, but she sets those to one side for later. She sets her twin acorn caps in front of her. She gathers some thick green leaves from a magnolia tree. The magnolia leaves have a brown side and a green side. She uses the brown to be the inside, and she gnaws the leaf to be the shape she needs, fashioning it, and stitching it into a pocket, one for each side of the twin acorn caps. She uses the burlap threads and the twine from vines to stitch the leaves into pockets, to be sewn onto the acorn caps. She mutters to herself, "Poking holes into the acorn caps is the most difficult part." She uses an old needle to poke holes only after she wraps her paws with cloth for safety.

Once her twin backpack sits before her, she knows she needs her sister and her mother to help fashion braided straps. She collects the three grapevine pieces and heads to one of her walls to reach for two little tubes which she uses to communicate with neighbors. She squeaks into two of the tubes which lead to her sister and her mother's homes, "Can you both come help me?"

Beth wears a big purple bow atop her head, and Mama Mouse wears a warm orange knit cap. Soon both her sister and mother stand ready to help. Making strong braided straps is a needed task, and it takes three of the mice to leap and criss-cross the vines into a firm braid.

"Beth, Mama Mouse." Betsy squeaks her hellos, hugging each one before beginning her instructions. Beth and Mama Mouse listen carefully, knowing Betsy could have changes in the process. "I need both of you to help me make a braid. Now each of us will hold a thin piece of grapevine. One, two, three, these are our spots," Betsy points to the ground in three spots. "I will be in the middle. Then one," she said, pointing at Beth, "you will hop with your vine into the middle, and then three," she says, looking at Mama Mouse, "you will jump into the middle, then I will, and then we start all over again until we have a braid."

Beth and Mama Mouse hold firmly onto their grapevine strands alongside of Betsy with her grapevine. "We're ready," Beth calls out.

"This ought to be so much fun," Mama Mouse squeaks. Mama Mouse, with a bit of a limp, still tries her best with no complaints.

"Go!" Betsy squeaks, and soon the braid comes after all the leaping and hopping. Benjamin stops what he's doing because he loves to watch the three of them make a braid.

"Oh dear," Betsy squeals. All three mice stop and look at the rather loose braid before them. "This will never do! I am so sorry!

I forgot, we must pull tightly after each jump, and then we will have a tight braid." Betsy chides herself, "I always seem to forget that when I give instructions."

"Never mind, dear. You'll soon have it right." Benjamin smiles and heads for the door to the outside.

"Oh, okay, Betsy, leap, pull, leap, pull, leap, pull. We'll get this right," says Beth while she carefully unravels the loose braid. The three mice giggle as they start leaping again, and Mama Mouse somehow keeps up with them since the pause-to-pull takes place. While they leap and giggle, Betsy tells Beth about the pecan husks and how baby beds can be made from them. "I could sure use some baby beds," Beth squeaks. Soon a beautiful tight braid sits on the floor before them.

"How lovely and tight our strap looks! Thank you both ever so much," Betsy says, hugging her sister and Mama Mouse. "Mama, you did so well, even with a hurt knee." Mama Mouse picks up both of her twig canes she'd gnawed for herself a few months ago. Mama Mouse snuggles each grandbaby mouse from the pine straw nest before rising up to go with Beth. "Oh, but first, let's have some tea, before you two head home," Betsy squeaks. The three mice ladies happily settle on a couch, sipping Earl Grey tea from tiny pretty teacups. All mice become quite quiet when enjoying cups of tea.

"We love coming over to help with your inventions," Mama Mouse squeaks as she heads to the path outside.

"Bye," calls Beth, adding "and thank you for telling me about the pecan husks as beds. I'll gather a few on our way home." Their chattering conversation sounds drift off as they walk along the brown dirt path towards their homes.

Just as Betsy washes up tiny cups, Benjamin bursts into the room. "Betsy! Just as you three began to rethink your strap, I hurried outside gathering some fall berries for our supper," he puffs and huffs many times, catching his breath, "and I was near Lady Dill's, so I gave her some of the medicinal roots she needs, and she was crying!"

Betsy gasps in disbelief, "Crying?" Benjamin nods, gasping for air, and Betsy stood silent, full of wondering and questions.

"It is nearly dark now," Benjamin squeaks. His tiny voice continues, "the owls will be out soon, not to mention coyotes and foxes. We must investigate further in the morning, and we can learn what happened."

Betsy nervously chews on one paw but squeaks, "I cannot wait until the morning when a friend is in need. I will stay clear of the owl and not crack one twig for him or any coyote or fox to hear."

Before Benjamin has a chance to voice his fear and protests, Betsy hurries out the door, holding a leftover magnolia leaf over her back as her shield of armor against all foes in the darkening night.

Chapter Four: Betsy Rushes Out

Betsy hurries along the paths towards Lady Dill's home as quietly and as quickly as she can, holding the thick magnolia leaf over her back. Betsy hopes the old owl is not awake yet or that perhaps the owl will think this is just a leaf blowing by. *I am nearly there,* she thinks, when a figure ahead looking a lot like Lady Dill startles her. The figure hurries as if she is ready to drop to all fours and run. She is wearing a torn pair of overalls, keeping her head down as she hurries along.

Once Betsy is closer, she can see this figure has all brown fur, just short fur, with the body the same outline in the darkness as Lady Dill. She nods to the brown-furred figure. *I wonder who that could be,* she ponders, but soon Betsy makes her way between the two boulders and along the path leading to Lady Dill's front door. Betsy lets herself in quietly and sees her friend. Lady Dill stands trembling, then moves restlessly about the room to her blue sofa and sits. Lady Dill keeps looking around her home, too, as if unseen things worry her.

Betsy sees her friend Dill not only wiping away tears but sees her shoulders shaking with sobs. "Oh, Dilly, my friend," Betsy squeaks.

Lady Dill hears Betsy's tiny voice of comfort, looking up. "Betsy! Oh, Betsy, the most terrible thing just happened!" Betsy hurries over closer to her friend. Lady Dill continues. "What a visitor I just had, looking about my own home, commenting on my three sofas, how that sofa could be perfect for herself, and that other sofa could be perfect for her grown son, and then the third sofa, perfect for her son's little ones, as if it was up to them to just move in without asking. Every Sunday afternoon, I love to have Fielding, my young rabbit friend, and her friends stop by for cake or cookies. If I turn over my three sofas to a scrounger, I feel I need to rearrange my entire life if several animals just move in."

"Oh, yes, scroungers do not think of the disruption to other animals' lives," Betsy comforts.

"I feel just miserable," says Lady Dill.

Lady Dill shakes with emotion, squeaking about how she loves her own home and uses her sofas for her visitors as well as herself, telling briefly of her home being torn apart earlier, adding a few mutters about "those blasted scroungers" and "why can't she go find her own place to live?" Lady Dill shakes her head no, no, no. "Of course, I care about helping others, but does that mean I must give up my own quiet, special home and have everyone move in?"

Betsy quietly listens as Lady Dill pours out her heartaches, "Look, she just came in without even a knock at my door, went about the room as if she's planning on moving in." Betsy nods, letting her friend talk through her feelings while she and Lady Dill

24

sit on the blue sofa together, comforted by each other's presence. Betsy decides not to mention the brown-furred animal she had just seen before arriving at Lady Dill's.

Lady Dill wipes away more tears, remembering to squeak, "Where are my manners? Oh, thank you, Betsy, for coming."

"Perhaps you ought to find a new home," Betsy squeaks. "I seem to recall this happened before. Scroungers tend to find an easily persuaded animal, someone they can charm into giving items to them, but why do they expect a free place to live?"

Lady Dill sobs with anguish, knowing someone she loves and cares for could still barge into her home. "Why ever do scroungers not think of the other person and how much love and helpfulness I feel. But that does not mean I can just let them take over my life." Her voice trails off into a sad, low tone.

Betsy squeaks quietly, "Why ever do they only want free this, free that, and not ever what can they do to help someone else?" Lady Dill shrugs her shoulders, not knowing why.

Lady Dill cries out a fervent squeak, "Why am I crying?"

"You are crying because this is what is left over, after a scrounger descends upon loved ones. You are crying because you are a caring, compassionate animal." Betsy gets the blue and green plaid quilt off the bed. The quilt has little purple fish on four of the corners. "You rest on the sofa and cover up with this quilt, good for comforting warmth." Lady Dill takes a deep breath, calming herself. Betsy tucks the quilt around Lady Dill. Warmth, friendship, and comfort bring rest, relaxation, and a new hope for Lady Dill.

"Hmm, you mention a new home? I think that might work. I can ask Rob, the rabbit who built my door, if there is a way it could be secure, because just this morning, someone came and tore the place apart," Lady Dill squeaks. "I should like to keep my handmade wooden door."

"Someone tore your place apart? Now I think you surely do need to move." Betsy patted her friend on the back. "I'm too small to help you move things, but I can still find ways to help you."

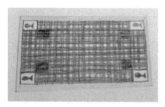

Betsy makes her way to the kitchen after seeing her friend Lady Dill is much calmer. Keeping busy seems to help, and she busies herself making a snack for her friend, Lady Dill. "Look at you, offering to help me, making me a snack, when you have eight little babies at home, plus all your backpack-making work," Lady Dill squeaks softly to her friend. "You are so dear to me, little Betsy."

Betsy squeaks, "Helping a friend is what I've seen in you, Lady Dill. Why, what about that tea tree oil for my own babies?"

Betsy hands a snack of apple slices on a carved platter to her friend. "Whatever comes, we will work through it, Lady Dill." They begin to munch some apple slices.

"Yes, we certainly will," Lady Dill answers. "I was just thinking, I can visit Rob and his wife, about my door, and maybe it would be good to also visit Ernest and his wife. I mean, she calls him Mr. Encyclopedia, and he is ever so clever. What if there is a way to be certain no one could barge into my home? I usually have animals knock first, but perhaps that is not quite secure for scroungers." The two friends giggle, and soon, plans are in the works for Lady Dill.

"You are welcome to sleep at my house and venture back to yours in the morning, Betsy," Lady Dill tells her.

Betsy squeaks to her friend, "I better rush home and help Benjamin with the babies, but thank you, dear Dilly." Betsy pulls the door shut tightly for Lady Dill. Betsy pulls the magnolia leaf over her back, and off she hurries into the darkness, this time in a different direction, towards her own home, full of thoughts of warmth, comfort, family, and love.

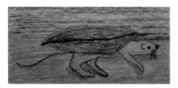

Chapter Five: Betsy and the Foundling

Betsy heads home after checking on Lady Dill, putting the thick magnolia leaf atop her back. She's traveling as quietly as she is able, but she hears some rustling and a tiny moan, so she freezes, listening intently. Ahead of her in the darkness, she sees a dug-out hole, and wiggling about in some leaves nearby is a chipmunk kit. It looks like a predator animal destroyed the chipmunk home, but this little one survived.

Betsy tosses away her magnolia leaf, gathering some oak leaves, wrapping up the chipmunk kit. "I guess your mama had an autumn litter," Betsy squeaks. "Come on, little one. You're about the size of my own babies." Even as Betsy cuddles the kit, the kit begins to nurse. In only a few minutes, the kit sleeps, and Betsy takes the foundling home. "Poor little thing. Everyone needs a mama, and you will be fine with my own little ones. Why, in just a few weeks, or at least after winter comes and goes, you'll be out there digging your own home."

Betsy rushes home under many bits of brush, even darting beneath sticker bushes in order to protect herself and the kit. A near-silent whoosh goes by overhead. Betsy lets out a loud squeal of terror as the owl swoops past her. She tosses a pebble which makes a plopping sound then the pebble scurries down a slight hill, making lots of small sounds as it rolls along its way. The noises grab the attention of the owl, so Betsy waits until she sees the owl flying in a different direction towards the new sounds.

Scurrying down into her hole, Betsy waits to call out to Benjamin until she is nearly at the base of their tunnel. "Benjamin, wait 'til you see!"

"How was Lady Dill? Did you find out anything? Wait!" Benjamin stares at the bundle in her arms.

"Look, Benjamin, a chipmunk kit. Some predator dug out their home, and I fear she is the lone survivor. She's had a tummy full of milk, so let me settle down with our eight to feed our own, and then we can talk about Lady Dill." Betsy rests on her side in the pine straw nest, and the babies crawl over to her side, nursing until one by one, they fall asleep with their new sister, the chipmunk kit. "What do you say we call her Chippy?"

"Oh, fine, dear, I like that name. Good-night, Miss Chips. In the morning, I'll begin teaching these babies all some manners of mice, but I believe she will fit in beautifully." Benjamin snuggles up next to his wife, and the family soon soundly sleeps.

With morning came feeding, then Benjamin divides up the babies into two groups. One group has a few large pinecones, damp ones, so the pinecones are all closed up. "Okay, so when you see these on the ground," squeaks Benjamin, "you sniff about and tear down the pieces, one by one, and try to find the seed that is hidden. When the pinecones are dry, they will open up, and seeds blow away." The four babies Benjamin has are Andrew, Brandie, Fawn, and Grayfur, divided so each parent has some mouselings to teach.

Betsy takes Hairy-Hazelnut, Chippy, Charlie, Dean, and Edward to a corner of their big room. She lays out five leaves. "Now all of you are growing fur fairly well now, so don't be telling me the floor is too cold." She tells them to sit still on their leaf for two minutes in a game she calls Quiet Mouse. "All animals such as mice and chipmunks must learn self-control. We will all sit quietly for two minutes." Squirming began, and Dean and Edward begin pushing a bit. "Now we must all start our two minutes from the beginning." Betsy merely points her paw at the two of them, and the look on her face seems to be enough to make them q-u-i-e-t, quiet. Betsy seems to be counting to herself, and sure enough, she squeaks, "Okay, good, that's about two minutes. That's pretty good. Tomorrow we will go for five minutes. I know you can do it. One never knows if a fox is nearby waiting for a meal."

Little Hairy Hazelnut, the youngest and runt of her litter, squeals a bit. "I don't want to be someone's meal, Mama."

"No, of course not, sweet Hairy Hazelnut, my lone creamy brown mouseling," Betsy squeaks in her coo of a mama voice.

"You, too, Chippy, you are also brown, so excuse me for saying 'my lone creamy brown'." Chippy smiles.

"Mama, she has stripes. I want some stripes, too," complains Hairy Hazelnut.

"Well, dear, that's not how it works. You be yourself, and she will be herself." Betsy nods sensibly to them all. "Now, each of you five get a different leaf please, in a quiet manner," with a bit of sternness in her face. "Charlie, Edward, Dean, be as quiet as mice in this game."

Each of the five hurried off quietly to get one leaf, and each returned to Mama Betsy. "Good job, now we will play hop to another leaf, and we will see which of you is a quiet mouse." Off to one end of the room, many jumps and hops happen, as babies must learn the importance of self-control, of quiet, and fairness to one another. "Look, I see a pine tree seed, fallen from one of those pinecones of your daddy's group," Betsy squeaked to her group. "Tomorrow, we shall play that game, but now, each of you can see what the seed looks like. Let your nose guide you to it."

Over on the other side of the big room, Benjamin has many rolling pinecones being chased by four mice. "Andrew, Grayfur, stop scurrying so fast! Brandie, Fawn! Stop!" Benjamin lets out a long sigh of tiredness. "This is a game of finding the hidden seeds, not a game of chasing pinecones around the home!" He tries again, "Forage! Use your noses! Sniff out that morsel! You can do it!" His four mouselings straighten back into behaving themselves, getting into their game, and Benjamin breathes out a big sigh as they begin munching at the seeds each one found. "Tomorrow, we will work on the quiet mouse game as well as the digging practice moves useful for tunneling."

Soon Benjamin and Betsy pass around some sunflower seeds, giving all nine babies time to learn how to use their teeth. At first, babies twirl the seeds in their paws, but finally one nibbles one end, sniffs the goodness inside, and the rest of the babies chew quickly into the seeds. All nine babies chew and chew, and Mama Betsy smiles contentedly, whispering to Benjamin, "Soon these nine will be off on their own in Corlett Caves somewhere, but for now, we can sit back and enjoy them while they're here with us." Benjamin cuddles up to Betsy, and he hands her some seeds to nibble.

"There is so much to teach them before they move off on their own," Betsy squeaks to Benjamin. He just nods quietly and lets out a big sigh as Betsy begins to list items, "How to wash laundry, how to fix a meal, how to be wary of snakes." Betsy squeaks further, "What a great danger snakes are for mice! Even if you are quiet and still, a snake may find you!" The mouselings and Chippy tremble in fear, clinging to each other and decide to listen more attentively to Betsy. Betsy remembers something, "Okay, Benjamin, we need to let the Patchers know about the foundling, just in case they know of any other survivors. We also need to tell them that Lady Dill has some distress, as well as having some items stolen earlier in the day." Betsy tells Benjamin what she knows. "I doubt if anyone survived in the chipmunk hole, after seeing it last night." Betsy sees Chippy wrestling with the baby mice, rolling about on the floor, giggling, and she feels all will be well with little Chippy.

The next morning arrives, and Benjamin and Betsy begin training their little ones a game called Find the Hidden Seeds before breakfast, when the mouselings and Chippy, or Miss Chips, as Benjamin calls her, are sure to be hungry. Mama Betsy and Benjamin sit in their chairs and watch contentedly at their large brood of youngsters. Benjamin quietly says, "Children grow up, we've learned to our sorrow, so quiet down, cobwebs, and dust, go to sleep. We're watching our babies, and babies don't keep." Betsy smiles, so fond of that saying from long ago.

Chapter Six: Fielding and the Patchers

The brilliant blue skies of September and October hurry autumn along on its course. The animals of Corlett Caves feel the colder weather coming, and cloudy skies with heavy rain follow, rushing along the change of seasons. Each sunny day comes with animals gathering and storing away food for the coming winter, and a few things happen as the animals pass one another through the paths in the forest.

News passes from animal to animal of Lady Dill's home disruption with some items stolen. Busy animals quickly go gathering and storing, going back out again to gather more, but scroungers do no gathering, no seeking of seeds to save for winter, no storing away items, and no working hard except maybe to work hard at doing nothing. Further news of a foundling rescued by Betsy passes from animal to animal throughout the Corlett Caves community. News reaches the Patchers, and a team is assigned and on their way.

Back in the area near her cave, Lady Dill stops her gathering of winter food stores and nervously heads back towards her cave to have her list of lost items ready to show the Patchers. Already the animals living near her have heard of her distressing day, and when out, each animal she meets along the paths asks her about her home being ransacked, what was missing, and about the chipmunk kit foundling Betsy found.

"Oh, yes, I wonder if they will keep the foundling and their young ones through the cold winter. Then they can all dig homes of their own in the spring." Lady Dill politely replies to all who inquire about her home disruptions and her missing items, "How kind of you to be asking about me." Lady Dill thinks, *surely the Patchers already know and will be coming to help me.* News

passes quite quickly through the forest, as animals out foraging tell news to other animals, and by the time Lady Dill reaches her home and sits down for her meal, a few of the Patchers knock on the wooden door of her home. This particular group has a rabbit, a squirrel, and a doe. The rabbit is a tall female with a light shade of brown fur. She wears a top with a side pocket for her pen, and she wears pants with a pocket for her notebook. Lady Dill recognizes her young friend, Fielding.

"Fielding! How wonderful! I am going to be making a nice cherry pie for our weekly time with your friends over here. I just happened upon a lovely bunch of cherries across the forest a bit."

"Oh, lovely, Lady Dll. I know Ella and a few of my rabbit

friends are looking forward to stopping by again," says Fielding. "Right now, we are here on a Patchers matter." Fielding gestured towards the squirrel who seemed to be the leader of the group. "Here's our leader, Ted."

Patchers are all sorts of species of animals. Beside the doe are the rabbit and a squirrel. Lady Dill welcomes them, inviting them inside. "Both of you come on in, and Miss Doe, I will leave my door open, so you can hear us. Thanks so very much for coming, and my, how quickly you came." Miss Doe, as the representative of speed for this particular group of Patchers, understands completely about waiting outside. She peers in the doorway, tucks her long legs beneath her, and settles down and chews while she listens.

Lady Dill leads the rabbit and squirrel into her home. Lady Dill knows many more animals are a part of Patchers. She knows she should listen carefully and then answer questions when asked for information. The squirrel dips his head politely, removing his hat. Lady Dill thinks, *I do so appreciate when a male takes off his hat when he enters a place. It seems so few males do this polite gesture.* Lady Dill feels relaxed.

The squirrel stands on his back feet and looks around carefully. "Thank you, Ma'am. We heard you're in need of assistance. My name is Ted, Ma'am." He chitters quickly and has such a cheerful look about him that Lady Dill feels a great sense of calm.

"Ted, thanks for coming by. News seems to have spread so quickly in this area," Lady Dills says.

The rabbit introduces herself, "Hello, Lady Dill. As you know, I'm Fielding, daughter of Rob, the carpenter. This is my first assignment, and I want to do all I can to help." Lady Dill likes her young friend, but this is the first time she has seen Fielding in an official capacity, so Lady Dill sees Fielding displaying an eagerness to help and efficiency in her speech, and Lady Dill listens with respect. Fielding smooths her clothes and smiles, and Lady Dill senses Fielding is full of questions. Fielding collects her notebook and her pen, and she is ready to jot down information.

"Fielding? You've joined the Patchers," Lady Dill says.

"Yes, Ma'am," Fielding replies. "I want to do something helpful in Corlett Caves with my life."

The squirrel chitters, "I know I've seen you, Lady Dill, as I go racing through the trees and forest looking for acorns, nuts, and seeds."

Lady Dill nods politely to Ted. "In my life, I have seen a black squirrel, a white squirrel, a few red ones in England, and ever so many gray squirrels such as yourself." *Oh, I think I need to be careful not to ramble on*, Lady Dill thinks. Ted takes control of the conversation.

"We understand you made a list of items we need to be looking for, and please give that to Fielding. As for the foundling, we feel a chipmunk baby can settle in with the mice family, as they are relatively the same in size, but our doe friend will be inquiring at any chipmunk homes she finds for a relative, as she travels farther across Corlett Caves' forest and fields. We know she can find many chipmunk families as she looks. From what we've heard so far, Betsy found the chipmunk home destroyed, but perhaps relatives can be found." Lady Dill listens carefully, waiting for any questions.

Fielding glances carefully about the home of Lady Dill while Ted speaks. Fielding speaks when Ted becomes silent.

"Lady Dill, we understand your home had been quite disturbed, and it looks quite put together now. Did you notice any paw prints? Can you remember how high did the damage reach? It gives us an idea as to the size of the animal responsible."

Lady Dill responds, "My, I hadn't thought of that. I feel as if the tallest spot of damage was this painting being removed." Lady Dill walks over to the painting and points up at its higher position above her own bed. Fielding follows, and she reaches upward with her front paws, stretching herself to get a perfect idea of how tall the intruder must be. Lady Dill hands the list of missing items to Fielding.

"Thank you, Lady Dill. Your information helps me a lot. I'll do my best to find your missing items . Let me see, a blue vase and some yellow pens. Plus, I'll keep an eye out for an animal who can reach as high plus who can lift such a painting." Fielding asks if she can stand up on the bed, excusing herself for needing to do so, but Lady Dill nods her approval, realizing that Fielding wants to lift the painting to see which animals might be able to lift it. Once Fielding hops off, she carefully smooths the quilts, and Lady Dill smiles. Fielding says, "This is going to help me a lot. Thank you."

Lady Dill looks at Fielding, "I'm afraid I cleaned up the muddy paw prints, but I know they look just like my own, except I never leave muddy paw prints around on my floors."

Fielding nods and says, "Oh, it must be of the same species as you, Lady Dill. It could be someone you know, some scrounger who has kept an eye on your home."

"Great thinking, Fielding," praises Ted the squirrel. "Let's get going now, and soon, one of us will be getting back to you, Lady Dill."

Lady Dill's face shows she suddenly remembers, so she asks, "Oh, one thing I need to ask you, Mr. Squirrel, sir. I had a scrounger burst into my home when I was here, after I had cleaned up my place. It distressed me or unsettled me, I should say."

"Oh, could you tell us more, please?" Ted asked.

Lady Dill rubs her paws together, as her emotions begin to return. She calms herself and explains, "She came for a visit, but then she was looking at my three sofas, saying she and her grown son and her son's babies could move in here, into my own quiet home, without asking." Ted and Fielding stood quietly listening, and they let Lady Dill continue. In a very weak squeak, Lady Dill added, "I was most distressed. Could it be related to the thief who entered and took items when the home lay empty?" Lady Dill wrinkles up her face, feeling she rambles on too much.

Ted scratches his chin and says, "Oh, yes, Ma'am, it could be that those two incidents are related. You most certainly need to ask someone to help you with a secure front door. Scroungers have no respect for the home of another animal. In fact, they may be opportunists, searching for someone as the next victim."

Fielding speaks up, "My father made that door, and I feel certain he could help. Plus, what about Ernest, the one we call Mr. Encyclopedia? He surely knows about locks." Fielding, Ted, and Lady Dill smile.

"Oh, he is so brilliant that when I ask him a question, he always says, 'it's really very simple' to me before he explains," Lady Dill squeaks.

Ted smiles and turns to his companions to say, "Come now. We'll leave Lady Dill to continue her autumn harvesting."

Lady Dill holds out her paw to shake each paw as the Patchers head to the door, and she squeaks happy thank you's to each one, saying, "Oh, I feel so much better," and, "You are all so efficient," and, "Fielding, please say hello to your father, Rob, and tell your sweet mother I hope to see her soon. She is such a dear friend of mine." Calling towards her doorway, Lady Dill adds, "Thank you, too, Miss Doe!" Having said their good-byes, the animals all begin making their way quickly down the path.

Lady Dill gathers her burlap bag, wraps her blue shawl around her shoulders, and tugs her door tightly shut. She hurries down the path to find more winter stores of food as every moment counts when preparing for winter. Soon Lady Dill hurries back along the paths towards her home, and she settles onto a sofa in her home, empty of visitors yet overflowing now with hope.

Chapter Seven: Ernest and Laney

The autumn winds pick up to swirl along through Corlett Caves, causing a continuation of the blanketing of the forest and fields with leaves of many colors. As Lady Dill walks through the blanket of leaves, she makes her way to the home of her rabbit friends, Rob and his wife, Claire. This colder day, Lady Dill wears a warmer coat of brown cloth with buttons up the front. Lady Dill carries in her front paws a small basket with a blue-checked cloth covering it. Feeling the top of the cloth, she feels the warmth of the carrot-flavored muffins.

This path to Rob and Claire's warren passes Ernest Encyclopedia and his wife Laney's warren, so besides carrying a basket of goodies, Lady Dill also wears a small backpack over her brown coat. Neatly inside are cookies made with sweetened mashed carrots, a particular favorite of her rabbit friends. "I hope

I don't get mixed up with cookies and muffins for my two families of rabbit friends," Lady Dill tells herself. "Muffins first, to Ernest and Laney, then cookies for Rob and Claire," she reminds herself.

At the edge of the forest, she comes to the opening of the home

of Ernest and Laney. Tall strands of thick grasses grow thickly as a barrier between the forest and the field, so this warren's opening is hidden from view to all but the animals. Lady Dill usually lets out a friendly call when visiting one of her friends, but Ernest has a string he rigged up long ago so that visitors could ring a bell far down in the warren simply by pulling on the string at the entrance.

Tugging on the string and listening until she hears a call from far below, Lady Dill smiles and makes her way down the curvy

path, following the tunnel's entrance to the warren. A slender brown rabbit with a white star on her chest greets Lady Dill, "Lady Dill, how good it is to see you!"

41

"Laney!" Both animals share a hug, and Lady Dill explains her door problem. Laney listens carefully.

"Oh, my dear, your home, torn apart!" Laney gives Lady Dill another hug. "Let me take your coat. Take a seat in this armchair." Laney pats the top of the armchair. "I'll call Ernest. He's just down further in his laboratory, but he's expecting your visit." Laney calls down to her husband.

Lady Dill calls out, "Oh, Laney, I have some muffins for you both." As Laney comes over to Lady Dill, the basket is opened. My backpack has something for Rob, Claire, and their little ones."

"Oh, how sweet you are," remarks Laney. "Let me get some napkins and tea started. You take a seat and rest a minute."

Calling out towards the kitchen, Lady Dill said, "Guess who I saw yesterday?" Without waiting for Laney to guess, she calls out, "Fielding! And my goodness, Laney, she is so poised, so smart, and I mean, she was thinking of things I had not thought of at all." Laney is familiar with Rob and his wife, Claire.

"I recall when Fielding was just a tiny little rabbit exploring the field and forest," Laney says.

"Me, too," Lady Dill adds. The friends begin catching up on the news, including the news of Lady Dill's home. "That's why I came by, Laney," she says to her friend. "I need to ask Ernest and you if there is any way I can make my home safe from thieves and scroungers."

Laney says, "I should hope so! Look, our tea is warm now, stay right there in that soft chair and you have your tea. I will go get Ernest," Laney hurries down further into the warren. Ernest comes up and promises to see the door of Lady Dill's home. Lady Dill thanks him and says her good-byes.

Soon she heads to the warren of her friends, Rob and Claire Rabbit, parents of Fielding. Her empty basket makes her smile, knowing the carrot muffins tasted just fine for Ernest and Laney. She carries in her front paws the empty basket with blue-checkered cloth. The cookies in her backpack will be moist and good to eat on this windy day.

Leaves swirl about Lady Dill, and the wind makes her fur above and below her brown coat fly in many directions, but she knows she will soon be at her dear friend Claire's cozy warren. Rob and Claire's warren opens up at the base of a red oak that looms high just inside the thicker part of the forest. With no string to pull, Lady Dill sees a brown wooden picket fence made from narrow sticks cut to the same lengths. Long vines weave through the narrow sticks to form a fence. Lady Dill sees a sign showing that a row of flowers for autumn is planted in a neat row. Nearby, yellow, orange, maroon, and purple chrysanthemums stand tall like cheerful soldiers in formation. Flat stones line up as a path towards the opening.

"How lovely!" Lady Dill calls out. All the grass within the confines of the brown picket fence has been carefully chewed short. "This makes me want a home not in a cave, so I can plant some flowers," Lady Dill squeaks. As Lady Dill walks along the stone pathway, she sees a little wooden mailbox. Lady Dill's cave has just a narrow crevice in the stone for mail. Lady Dill chides herself and longs to fix her home now, so she can have a happier time with letters and a garden as well as visitors she already enjoys. Just as Lady Dill ponders her own home, out from the warren's opening comes Fielding.

"Fielding! How nice to see you again."

"Oh, hi, Lady Dill. I was just visiting Mom and Dad this morning. My home is about fifteen trees' distance that way." Fielding points. "I am actually heading to ballet class, and then I have a few Patchers meetings over the next few days. I think I figured out some things about your thief, so I will stop your place soon, if that's okay." Fielding seems to be in a hurry, so Lady Dill smiles and tells her how amazing this news is for her to hear, calling out her thanks.

Lady Dill smiles and heads to the warren opening. A little knob of wood twirled, rattling against another bit of wood, and as Lady Dill plays with it, she realizes this is the ingenious doorbell without a bell, but it's a doorbell just the same, all made of wood. "How clever this family is!"

Faintly a call of "Help me! Please, somebody, help me," rises and swirls across to Lady Dill's ears. She quickly turns around, tilting her head slightly to improve her hearing so she can determine the call's location.

"Yes, I hear you! Call again!" she squeaks, and another call came.

"Help me! I feel so sick! I'm here, beneath the tall grasses."

Knowing the tall grasses grow at the edge of the forest, Lady Dill backtracks, and the calls continue, helping to guide her. "Oh, my dear, whatever happened?" Lady Dill kneels down next to a young weasel who is frightened, vomiting a bit, with fear in her eyes. The little weasel tries standing up.

"The world is turning, turning, always to my left," she calls out to Lady Dill. With each movement of her head, the little weasel vomits a bit more, groaning and wiping her face. "What's happening to me? I'm scared! I don't think I can walk until this spinning stops!"

"Oh, my dear youngster, hold your head as still as you can." Lady Dill calmly gets out her blue-checkered cloth and wipes the weasel's face clean. "It seems that your tummy gets upset with

44

movements, so I think holding your head as still as you can might help."

The weasel moans a bit but keeps as still as she can. Clearly, she feels scared as her world spins so violently. She opens her eyes and shuts her eyes, over and over until saying, "When I open my eyes, the world is spinning so!" She groans a bit.

"Okay, I understand. Shut your eyes and keep them shut. I know someone who is an expert in this field. I must get you to Dr. Watford." Lady Dill wants to ease the fear of the weasel, so Lady Dill squeaks softly in a calm voice, "Don't you worry a bit, little gal. Tell me your name, honey."

A weak voice says, "Daisy."

Lady Dill explains, "Daisy, you just settle back and lie down in the soft leaves with your eyes shut. Dr. Watford is about the kindest doctor ever, and he is quite knowledgeable on what is happening to you. No problem, sweet girl." The weasel keeps her eyes shut now, since it calms her for her eyes to not see the world turning. Lady Dill wonders how will she get this weasel to Dr.Watford, and she knows she still needs to ask Rob and Claire about her door. How can a sick weasel be moved without the process upsetting her stomach again?

Lady Dill, so full of questions, tries to work through each issue. "My door can wait," Lady Dill squeaks.

"What door?" young Daisy says.

"Oh, I didn't mean to say that out loud, but sometimes I think out loud, I guess. I am going to take you straight to rabbit Dr. Watford. I am thinking about what items I need, items to help me get you there. Hmmm," Lady Dill squeaks. She unbuttons her brown coat, removes it, then buttons it back up. "I have an idea. I'll put two poles into the sleeves, you can stretch out right onto the top of my coat, and I can pull you right over to his office." She sets it all up, but something is not right. "Oh dear, this needs some rethinking. The coat can't hold anyone this way. You'd slide right off."

Lady Dill soon had two poles, inserting them instead into her buttoned-up coat, and seeing the sleeves just dangle, she helped the little weasel onto the coat. "Be sure to keep your eyes closed,"

she reminds Daisy. After Lady Dill reworked things, she squeaks happily, "Now this seems to be a much better travois! I can pull you along quite well. We'll just use the sleeves to tie you in place."

"Trav, trav-vwaa?" Daisy said.

"Yes, sweetie. Travois. Imagine you are a Native American long ago, and you want to carry things. It's a French word, t-r-a-v-o-i-s, with the letter S silent."

"Okay," Daisy said softly, adding, "Keeping my eyes shut is helping."

"Oh, how brave you are, sweetie." Looking about, Lady Dill gets her bearings and heads back into the forest. To keep little Daisy from worrying, Lady Dill tells her about rabbit Dr. Watford's adventurous mountain climbing trips.

"This ought to work much better," Lady Dill repeats to Daisy. Lady Dill continues making turns right and left, down hills, around boulders, pulling the travois behind her, until she reaches the part of the forest where the doctors have their places of business.

The animals at Dr.Watford's office help to write down the name and symptoms of the little weasel. Lady Dill can tell this young weasel is newly moved out on her own. "I am going to sit with you, and after he sees you, I will help you get back home if necessary. No worries, now. Dr. Watford is really kind. He will know what to do." Lady Dill notices Daisy lets out a big sigh of relief.

"Thank you for helping me, Ma'am. I think the worst of it has passed. It will be a relief to find out what is the cause." The little weasel rubs her face with a damp cloth from the office staff. "What's your name, Ma'am?"

"Oh, it is not a problem to help you, Daisy! I'm Lady Dill. You're going to enjoy feeling better. I am sure Dr. Watford will understand what's been happening."

Lady Dill and the little weasel sit in the waiting room. Someone leads them back to a room to wait for the doctor. Rabbit Dr. Watford enters, he shakes the paws of Daisy and smiles at them both. Dr. Watford is tall, wearing black shiny shoes on his back paws and a nice suit. Dr. Watford asks Daisy what is wrong, and he listens carefully to her symptoms. Then he explains what is happening inside Daisy's ears, deep inside her head, to cause her world to spin. He points at charts on the wall of the inner workings

47

of ears. Daisy relaxes right away, and soon she understands more about the cause of her world spinning. Lady Dill notices how kind and caring he is to the little weasel, Daisy.

"Thanks so much, Dr. Watford, sir," says Daisy. "I never knew we have inner ears. I am so glad all that spinning has stopped. I am so glad to learn that it will not last long. Thank you for the medicine to help my ear calm down."

Lady Dill reminds Dr. Watford to be careful when he is dangling off of cliffs when out on his adventures. "We sure need animals like you, helping so many of us with such knowledge, so you take care." Dr. Watford smiles and thanks them for coming.

"It is so wonderful to have animals who've learned so much and then turn it into a way of helping others," Lady Dill squeaks to Daisy on their way out.

"Yes, that's so true, Lady Dill. I guess he stayed in school and learned a lot, to be able to help animals like that, didn't he?" Soon Daisy is back to her hollow log where she has her home. She digs up some buried food for herself. She tells Lady Dill thanks, and as she digs up her food she says, "We weasels never eat someone else's food, but we do bury our own food to dig it up later."

"Well, I didn't know that, Daisy," Lady Dill squeaks. "You take care, and I will head off to my friends' home now."

"Bye, Lady Dill, and thank you again for helping me! I know I can get home quickly now. Don't forget to get your coat," Daisy calls out.

Chapter Eight: Rob and Claire

Once back at the brown woven twig picket fence of her friends' home, Lady Dill lets herself through the gate, rattling again the inventive wooden doorknob, hearing it clatter in cheerful sounds. Soon Rob appears with Claire slightly behind him. Claire wears a pretty necklace with silver and blue. Rob wears a worker's apron and has wood shavings on it.

Greetings to each other are soon calling back and forth, "Lady Dill," and "How pleasant to see our old friend."

Lady Dill says, "Oh, how good it is to see you both again!"

Rob asks, "How's that door working out? What's this about an intruder?"

Lady Dill nods her head yes, squeaking, "That's what causes me to come seek your help, but also, may I order one of those nice wooden mailboxes? And I just adore your brown twig fence!" Lady Dill hugs her dear friend, Claire, saying, "Claire, it has just been too long, and I'd like to write letters, so we can keep in touch easily when winter sets in."

Claire agrees, "I love writing letters. It would be so wonderful to hear about your days, to not have to wait until spring or summer when visiting friends is much easier."

Lady Dill squeaks, "You have such pretty necklaces, Claire. Let me look at the front and the back of it. I need to take more effort with myself." Lady Dill tries smoothing her fur in an effort to improve her appearance. She looks carefully at both sides of the sparkling blue necklace with copper wire on both sides.

"Thank you. My daughter made this necklace for me, and I love it so. Your brown coat looks so warm," says Claire.

"Oh, it is growing quite windy outside, and my fur gets so windblown," Lady Dill squeaks.

The gusts of the autumn winds began to catch hold of the three friends, blowing fur every way possible, sending chills to each of them.

"Let's get down in the warren. There's nothing like an underground home," Rob says. Off they head, down, turning, then down further, then another turn past a storage room, past a work room, past a storage room with various pieces of wood, down and further down until a big room opens up before the three of them.

Looking around, Lady Dill sees a blue chair and heads towards it. "Here is my favorite spot!"

Rob and Claire both start to chuckle, knowing as friends do, what pleases each other.

"Okay, I am going to get some warm cocoa going." Claire heads to the far corner where her kitchen area is set up.

Rob takes a chair near Lady Dill and says, "We just had someone using our knocker before you did, but when we went up, no one was there."

Before he could continue, Lady Dill squeaks, "I am afraid that was me, just before I had a weasel in dire need of help, so I hurried to take her to Dr. Watford."

"Oh, good. I know he does amazing work and understands the inner workings of almost every animal," Rob says. "What can I do to help you with the door? Word came about a few problems with animals getting inside of your home; is that correct?"

"Oh, my goodness, I sort of have two different problems, and by the way, your daughter, Fielding is just so amazing. She is researching and locating my items that went missing, and I feel I don't have to worry about those missing items, except I still do need help keeping my home shut up tightly when I go out on my errands. I even had someone walk right in on me without knocking, wanting to move right on in." Lady Dill gives a bit of a shrug. "My husband and I worked hard to find a cave where we raised our young. I need my home for my business with herbal medicine. I cannot start having scroungers forcing their way to live in my own home."

Lady Dill, Rob, and Claire all thought quietly about the issue, as it was hard on everyone to deal with scroungers. "One never wants to see this type of thing, yet it is scroungers we know and love who seem the most difficult. We feel love for them, but -." Lady Dill did not know how to say what she feels, "--somehow I am left feeling guilty for wanting and needing my own quiet home."

"Yes, Lady Dill, I think many of us in Corlett Caves do not feel any sense of calmness or even what the proper response ought to be towards scroungers, and it is always worse when we know and love them. They don't seem to realize the turmoil that follows."

Claire brought over three mugs of steaming cocoa, and each took a mug into their cold front paws. "I can never understand why they do not figure out their own homes as soon as they leave their own parents," says Claire.

"It is such a good thing, to have a calm home of my own," squeaks Lady Dill.

With a mug of cocoa in his paws, "Ahh," said Rob.

"Thank you, Claire," says Lady Dill.

"Yes, honey, this warms me right up," says Rob to Claire.

Claire smiles and says, "This cocoa is perfect with the howling winds outside. I do think winter will be here soon. We might even get snow this year."

Lady Dill responds, "Oh, you might be right, and we ought to check with our weather animal muskrat. Once the muskrats and river rats build their winter quarters by the riverbank, we can check on how thickly they make their walls."

"Yes, how right you are!" Claire agrees.

Just then, two toddler rabbits came hopping out into the main room. "Mommy, Kenny and I are hungry now," calls one of them. Claire cuddles the two little rabbits while Lady Dill coos about how adorable they are,

"My, how precious! I didn't know you had some autumn babies! Hi, Kenny, hi sweetie," she squeaks. "I'm Lady Dill."

"I am Emma," the little rabbit says while fluffing her pink dress. "Mommy, Kenny and I want some food now."

Lady Dill suddenly remembers her cookies in her backpack. "Oh, Emma! That reminds me, I brought some carrot cookies!" Lady Dill reaches for her backpack, adding, "They might be a bit squished, because they were in an adventure today." The little rabbits drink from carrot-shaped sippy cups.

"What adventure?" asks little Emma.

Soon Lady Dill explains to Emma and Kenny about the weasel who had been so overcome with the whole world spinning.

Claire gathers some tidbits for her rabbit young, and she brings over two little dishes. Lady Dill hands each little one a cookie, and she offers some to Rob and Claire, then she takes one for herself. "Goodness, it came out just right, that's all of them gone!" Lady Dill says she sure loves it when that happens. Little Emma munches away at her cookie, using her hands in such gentle, feminine motions as she talks to the visiting Lady Dill. Kenny, the smaller of the two, lowers his food pieces into a mashed carrot dip then munches his food, listening quietly to all the chatter that follows about doors and keeping strangers out of homes and what a mess Lady Dill found.

Kenny and Emma's fur glistens in a light shade of soft brown. Lady Dill smiles and says, "Kenny, with your white star on your forehead, you look like a little cinnamon star!"

"Kenny, you're a star!" Emma hugs her little brother and tells Lady Dill, "Kenny, him not talk much, but he understands everything we say." Lady Dill smiles, loving Emma's beginning English.

Once the little ones sit playing on the floor, Rob comes with some samples of his latching mechanisms. "It is a sad thing that thieves are ready to grab and go, and between Ernest and I, I can make you a doorway, so that any bolt Ernest has on hand can then fasten carefully into the doorway and be most secure. We'll stop these intrusions."

Lady Dill asks, "Rob, thank you, and I just love the fence you made outside, and I really love the flowers, Claire. I will be digging myself a new home, as hard a job as that will be this autumn, but I will dig quickly before winter sets in. Then I could begin spring by making a garden, and a fence is like a dream item to me. My head is so full of ideas now!"

Claire perks up as she hears this idea. "What a good idea, Lady Dill. You can't affix a latch of some sort on a wooden door of a home in solid rock. I feel certain you can dig a soft earthen home, and Rob can make you a wooden doorway."

"One drawback, Lady Dill, that you must consider, is that if you have an earthen home, that animal you mentioned may come and start to dig herself a room. At least in the stone, she cannot dig to expand the space." Rob always helps by thinking of every option to consider.

"Well," Lady Dill says, "I am going to give her my cave home. Or maybe it could be set up for anyone who needs a safe place for a night or two." Lady Dill smiles.

54

Rob's brow crinkled up as he scratched his chin. "I think that's a tremendously good idea!"

Claire begins to fidget, so Lady Dill knows Claire wants to say more, so Lady Dill looks at her friend and nods. "Oh, just think, Lady Dill, you can have a room separate for your bed and your books, and you can have a separate room for all your medicinal supplies, then the big room for your kitchen, your couches, your lamps, and your painting. I'm so excited." Lady Dill begins to giggle a bit.

Emma came hurrying over to Lady Dill. "Can I help dig? Look at Kenny, him have good feet for digging, and me, too!" She held up one of her back feet, long and made for digging.

"Awww, what can I ever do without such kind and helpful friends? Yes, Emma, you can help me dig, and Kenny, too, and you know what?"

"What?" says Emma.

"I'll dig a room just for visiting little ones, and I'll keep toys in it," Lady Dill explains.

Emma hops right into Lady Dill's arms then hurries to hop in her mother's arms, "Oh, I'm so 'cited! Kenny, him not talk much, but him happy, too!" Lady Dill smiles at Emma and praises her for her beginning English, finding it so adorable to hear.

Rob, Claire, Lady Dill, Emma, and Kenny all smile with eagerness about a new home for Lady Dill, with a mailbox for letters, a picket fence, flowerpots, and a special toy room. "I will leave a note for Ernest on my way back home."

Lady Dill begins writing, knowing she must hurry home before the darkness of night.

The note reads: *Dear Ernest, I've decided I will dig a new home and reuse that wooden door. I look forward to seeing you about how I can best keep my home secure, and perhaps you can let me know if this door will work. Rob crafted it for me, and I really would love to keep it. Thanks, Lady Dill.*

Lady Dill folds up the note and places it in her backpack.

"Here, take these burlap bags for packing items," says Claire, handing her a stack of folded bags.

"Oh, thanks so much, Claire," Lady Dill squeaks. Slipping into her coat, fastening it, and holding onto her basket, wearing her backpack filled with folded bags, she thanks her friends again and heads towards her home nestled between the boulders in Corlett Caves. What a nice ending it is to have a cheerful beginning ahead.

Chapter Nine: Solutions for Lady Dill

Lady Dill hurries up to Ernest and Laney's warren door, setting her note into the opening and tugging the rope Ernest has for his doorbell, but Lady Dill doesn't stop to wait, for she knows she must hurry homeward. Already she hears the "whoo, whoo" of an owl in the distance, so she stays as quiet as she is able, dodging quickly past any open areas. She sees mice scurrying past in their own business of rushing home. Birds seem to be in their nests already. A few bats swoop about in the open spaces, eating bugs that fly through the coming dusk and darkness.

Seeing her two boulders ahead, Lady Dill scoots herself down the brown soft dirt path towards her home, squeezing between the boulders, happy to be home. She hangs up her backpack as she enters. Looking about the room, for the first time in all the years she has lived in her stone home, she sees it as a place to say good-bye to, and she pats the gray walls, grateful that this has been home. She thinks, *sometimes, it is good to just move on. Someone else can make their home here.* Lady Dill craves a garden, a twig picket fence, a toy room, a library, a spot for her bedroom wall unit, and of course, her living room with the kitchen to one side.

Lady Dill puts up her coat and sets about to prepare herself some food and a cup of fresh water to drink.

As she nibbles at her supper of seeds and berries, she thinks about a new home, and with digging being her way of making a new home, she gets to jotting down ideas and sizes she thinks each room could be. Yawning soon has her ready to clean up and head off to slumber away after she tucks a blue and purple quilt about her.

Drowsily she thinks about tomorrow, *I shall see Fielding, Claire, Emma, little quiet Kenny, and I'll see Ernest, Claire, and Betsy and cuddle little Chippy and the mouselings. They will love that I will have a toy room. All the little ones should stay through most of the winter. Emma, Kenny, Chippy, and each of those eight little mice, I want to know their little personalities. They're the future of Corlett Caves,* she thinks. Off she drifts into dreamy times of sleep.

By the time the first knock comes to her door the next morning, Lady Dill has put her books into a few backpacks. The burlap bags Claire loaned her are now filled with items. Her medicinal plants take more time, but she is nearly halfway through categorizing them with labels, carefully wrapping each into thick brown paper, tied up with strings. Lady Dill opens the door to see Fielding with a few of her friends, so Lady Dill greets them with a bright smile,

"Hi, Fielding, how nice of you and your friends to come by. It's great to see you again. Please remind me of the names of your friends."

"Well, Franklin is down by Ella, and she is here next to me, and Trevor is wearing green today," Fielding says. All four rabbits stand taller than Lady Dill amongst the greenery in the forest.

"We all went to school together. Ella wants to design clothing. She makes a lot of clothes for us. Trevor and Franklin, both like to figure out things and to explore, the same as Ella and I. All three of them are thinking about joining the Patchers," Fielding says, nudging one of the friends near her, hoping one would speak up.

"Oh, yeah, that's right. I need some adventure in my life, or I'll stay home sewing endlessly," Ella says.

"Oh, adventure is great for young adult animals, and how wonderful that would be," says Lady Dill. "I want to bring the generations together, so in light of that, I wonder, could you four come around and visit about 4:00 every Sunday afternoon? I plan on having little Ms. Chips come, too, and she and I will look forward to our get-togethers each week. I will bake a cake each week, and we can share a pot of tea between us."

"Oh, terrific," Franklin says with a big smile. "Food!"

"Do you mean we will meet with old folks on purpose?" whispers Trevor. Ella hops over to him and jabs him with her elbow.

"Shh," Ella whispers.

"We'd like to meet with you and visit, Lady Dill," says Ella.

59

Fielding quickly agrees with Ella, hoping Lady Dill did not hear Trevor. Fielding scratches her chin, whispering to Ella, "Surely her cakes and kindness will win Trevor over. Besides, Patchers help all generations."

Ella nods to Fielding.

"Lady Dill," Fielding says, "Ella, Franklin, Trevor, and I were talking about the scroungers, and with winter coming, we thought maybe the animals of Corlett Caves would be willing to donate any extra food, so some Patchers could set up a meals area."

"Oh, what a good idea!" Lady Dill says.

Franklin agrees, "Yes, and all four of us had a great baker from our high school, and she made the best rolls. We thought we'd ask her to be in charge, because she worked in our cafeteria at school."

"Yes, her name is Ms. Ann, and she is really a good cook, for sure," Trevor says, remembering the delicious rolls. "I think when animals come to help you move, we could tell them about Ms. Ann and see who can donate and help."

"How smart all of you are, and how helpful this will be," says Lady Dill. "Now on Sundays, when you four come, be sure to bring some friends," Lady Dill adds. "I like it when I get to know the younger generations."

"Except that old folks tend to be stuck in their ways," Trevor mutters softly to Ella.

Ella jabs him in the side, hoping to shush him.

Fielding speaks up, "Yes, Ma'am. We sure will. It is so nice of you to have us for cake, so we'll be sure to come after you're settled into your new home." Getting right to the matter of importance, she digs some things out of her backpack. "Here is your blue pitcher and your yellow pens, from your list."

Lady Dill gasps, "Wow! How did you find these? Where were they? Did you find out who took them?" Lady Dill stops herself from asking another question because she feels she is already asking too many questions.

Franklin speaks up, "She did the coolest thing. She went to where scroungers tend to try to sell stolen goods, and she kept a special watch. I wish I could've been there."

Fielding smiles and says, "Yes, Ma'am, I found these by checking out other animals with paw prints like you described. I thought perhaps the one who took these items would show them to some friends, and sure enough, the particular animal did just that. Sometimes thieves are kind of dumb."

Lady Dill giggles and says, "I can see the future is in good hands with you four as Patchers."

Fielding says, "The animal was out in the middle of a wooded area, showing these items as her most precious items, but as soon as I asked her about your home, she dropped everything and ran off! It was the fastest I have ever seen an animal such as her move, right down on all fours in a flurry of furry paws moving fast!" Fielding giggles, and Lady Dill joins in.

"Oh, Fielding, I am so glad you are my assigned Patcher! Surely you are meant for great things," Lady Dill praises her.

"Oh, I nearly forgot. My boss says it's official. Betsy can care for the foundling chipmunk, being the same size, more or less, as the mouselings. It seems to be just a few weeks until winter sets in, so it would be most appreciated if they could see Chippy, little Ms. Chips, as you like to call her, through the cold winter until she is eager to go find her own home." Fielding smiles, knowing that is exactly when she felt she was ready to move on, away from childhood and into being a young adult on her own.

Lady Dill pauses, almost afraid to ask more, but she knows she needs to know. "Fielding, who do you think wrecked my home? I mean, I know it is an animal of my species, as you said the other day, because the paw prints match ones I make when outside on muddy paths. I'm afraid to ask, because I know of one who later came by to check out my home, perhaps to investigate whether she could move right on in." Lady Dill sighs, quite glad she mentioned her question.

"Yes, Ma'am, I am sorry to say, the one I saw with your grandmother's blue pitcher and your yellow ink pens, she is the same one you told us about." Fielding sees Lady Dill exhale a loud, sad sigh.

After a long pause, respecting Lady Dill's sadness, knowing it to be someone loved by Lady Dill, Fielding stands quietly and gives Lady Dill a gentle hug.

"Thank you, sweet Fielding. I'll be okay. I am going to be digging myself a new home, so if that scrounger is homeless, my cave home is going to be a free home. There will be a happy future somewhere else for me. I hope to see you again. You impress me, and I especially like your kindness," Lady Dill tells her.

"Thank you, Ma'am, and you call me if ever you need the help of a Patcher." Fielding heads out the door, down the soft dirt path, and out into the wooded area. Lady Dill pulls her wooden door shut and begins setting her kitchen items into one area. Another knock on her door announcing another visitor brings Lady Dill to her door again.

"Oh, Ernest, thank you so much for coming," Lady Dill says to the tall rabbit. He wears a navy-blue vest and has a pair of glasses that slide down continually to the edge of his nose. He nods his hello without speaking and looks carefully at the door, behind it, along the edge of it, and at the entire area near the door. "Ernest, do you think there's a way to secure the door at my new home? Is it something I could get? I mean, I know I cannot make one, but perhaps someone can, and I could buy it. Oh dear, I ramble on so."

Ernest keeps looking at the door and begins asking questions about her move, when she wants to move, and he looks about her home, saying to himself, "Hmmm, let me get an idea about how many items you have, for packing up," and "which ones are too heavy for andher to lift." He kept asking questions, "let me see, how many animals will we need?" Then he asked Lady Dill, "Have you begun to dig yet?"

Lady Dill squeaks, "No, sir, I'm packing up and dividing up things, and I think I plan on starting my digging tomorrow. A few friends promise me they'll be coming." Ernest and Lady Dill talk about how many rooms she needs, and Lady Dill shows Ernest sketches.

"I see your three sofas have the pegs to take them apart, and so they will be easy to move. I do promise my wife and I will move this door tomorrow, and if you can spare it for the day, we will carry it to my workshop and affix a proper bolt on it. I find many in the patios and porches, and some even beneath the porches, long forgotten by humans, and completely unused. Rob can make anything out of wood, so he can come to my workshop, see the door, and measure out what he would need for making a doorway, so the bolt has something secure to fit into."

"My, I don't understand how all that works," Lady Dill says, yet knowing that of course, Rob and Ernest know their jobs well. "I'm so grateful."

"It's really very simple," Ernest says, and Lady Dill immediately smiles, knowing he always says that about topics which are complicated for everyone else.

"Thank you, Ernest. You are such a help. I'll bake you a carrot pie, just as soon as my new kitchen is up and working," she tells him, knowing that rabbits cannot resist carrot pie.

"Oh, well, if we're talking carrot pie, that will be payment in full as far as I am concerned! I'll be telling Rob about this door, so there is no need to wait on him to visit today. He can measure the door from my warren tomorrow." Ernest shakes her hand in a gentlemanly way and takes his leave. Just as he was about to pull her door shut for her, he calls out, "I shall bring six tall rabbits to move your sofas and shelves and bed wall unit in pieces, once your home is built, and many a rabbit will come help dig if needed, as soon as you know your location."

Lady Dill gasps with glee, "Oh, Ernest! I'm so thrilled. Thank you, kind sir!"

She hurries out into the brisk autumn air to go find a location for her new home.Lady Dill thinks, *I will pass on this cave home to that scrounger, as she seems to need a home of her own. It brought my husband and me a safe place to live.*

Hurrying down the brown paths with the sunshine twinkling down between the branches of the bare leaves and down between the green of the evergreen trees, Lady Dill hurries with hope and an eagerness for her own new beginning. She thinks about the scrounger, loving her yet not understanding her: *I wish her well and a happy life, and maybe somehow, she will make it.* Corlett Caves is a good place to live, and maybe I can think of a way to help those who need more help. Lady Dill heads out of sight.

Chapter Ten: New Beginnings

The next morning, Lady Dill hurries past the red oak where Betsy and Benjamin live. Lady Dill drops a hastily written note down their tunnel with the note saying:

Dear Benjamin and Betsy, babies, and little Chippy, Please come tomorrow to the big live oak in the field past the rabbit warren of Rob and Claire. I am digging a new home today and wish to invite you tomorrow to join me. Fondly, Lady Dill.

She turns north towards the homes of the rabbits with the warrens dug deep downward in the soil. She thinks she wants her home to be near Betsy and her rabbit friends, so she can visit each with ease. She slows her pace and looks about at the trees. Just near the edge of the forested area is a large field with a massive live oak with its branches reaching so far on either side.

Live oaks grow in warmer climates, and they offer homes to variety of animals. Squirrels chatter their hellos down at Lady Dill. A raccoon is high in the tree. Birds of many types fly about through the tree. Lady Dill sees something twinkling, scattered about in the tree, but maybe she imagines those sparkles. Lady Dill shakes her head and shrugs her shoulders, then she looks carefully around the base of the huge trunk. She cannot believe no one has a home near this gorgeous tree. Seeing no holes, she hangs up her clothing nearby.

Lady Dill feels a bright sense of hope, even with the cold blasts of air warning her and the other animals that winter is shortly coming to Corlett Caves. She is full of happy thoughts, *I shall dig as fast as my digging paws will allow, for I know I can dig it with hard work. What a special tree with branches far reaching to the sides. I will love living here, where I can see it each time I go outside.* Lady Dill decides to get started right away on this new autumn morning. She heads to the far end of the massive tree trunk, so her entrance can be out of the view of any humans. She begins to dig.

Furiously Lady Dill digs and digs and digs, and she makes a turn in her main entryway, a medium-sized room for any water that comes downward, and then she reverts back to the main tunnel with a slight upward dig before turning her tunnel downward again, just so that any water will go down into the holding area and not down into her main areas. Soon she has a room for her coats and shawls close to her entry. She digs a room for her bed further down, and she digs a room for her new toy room which she knows ought to be off her living room and kitchen. She makes sure her tunnel is wide enough for rabbits to bring in her sofas.

Next, she digs her largest room for her sofas and kitchen. Since that is her biggest room, she shoves dirt behind her, up the tunnel and out of her main tunnel. She pats down the freshly dug dirt all around the base of the holly bush, so no one coming by will suspect an animal's home is nearby. Back down her tunnel she hurries. The dirt feels soft against her paws. She feels so glad that lots of autumn rain softens up the earth. Once winter comes, this dirt will be so hard and quite difficult to dig.

Before dusk is near, she hurries back to the cave home and begins bringing her belongings to her new home. Once she has moved all she is able to carry alone, she washes in the Corlett

Caves hot springs, She hurries back to her new home and tucks herself to bed with her blue and green quilt.

Early the next morning, eight tall rabbits come by and are soon carrying her sofas, tables, lamps, and piles of clothing and shawls. "Oh my, thank you so much," she squeaks, seeing so many of her friends with arms full of their babies or of her things. Fielding shows up with a skill at organizing, so once the tall rabbits have the shelves and cubby holes in place, Fielding starts right in with the job of organizing the books, herbal cures, roots, mortar and pestle, and a stack of bowls. She even places the mountain painting up over Lady Dill's bed. "Oh, Fielding, I'm so grateful to you."

Lady Dill washes off her paws and settles onto her blue sofa, resting, and Beth, Mama Mouse, and many friends and little ones come by to help arrange pillows on the sofas and chairs, books on the bookshelves, and a few dishes in the kitchen. They left all the rest of the items for Lady Dill to arrange after her needed rest.

Fielding and Ella come to Lady Dill with an idea. "Lady Dill, Ella and I were thinking more about collecting donations and about Ms. Ann and her tasty bread and meals. We could see if some of the animals want to help make a sort of earn-a-meal day, where they could eat after any chore is completed. Animals who do not have enough to eat could have a good meal on the special meals day." The two younger rabbits look eagerly at Lady Dill.

"What a wonderful idea!" Lady Dill thought for a minute, then she exclaimed, "I remember Ms. Ann from the watering hole. I feel certain we can add in this idea of yours: do a chore to earn a meal."

"Yes, Ma'am," Ella says. "Trevor and Franklin are already making lists of chores that would be helpful in Corlett Caves," she adds. "Trevor has been putting up some signs, too."

"Great ideas. We have a nice community here, and lots of helpfulness is going to help us all. I really like the idea of a chore in exchange for a meal," Lady Dill says.

"Lady Dill, I didn't know you knew Ms. Ann. Isn't she the rabbit with light brown fur who sings those country music songs?" Fielding asks.

"Yes, that's my friend, Ann, from the watering hole." Lady Dill

smiles. "There's a hot water spring underneath, so the water gets quite warm for senior animals. We have an exercise class in the water," Lady Dill tells the other rabbits.

"I have seen that class, and it looks like a class of synchronized exercises, only it's in warm water," Ella adds.

"Yes, that watering hole is full of helpful people who might want to help out. Maybe these scroungers and those less fortunate will begin to enjoy their lives more with the added friendships and food," Lady Dill says.

Fielding and Ella move to begin unpacking items for Lady Dill, just as newer visitors arrive.

In the tunnel come Benjamin, Betsy, Chippy, and the eight baby mice, so Emma and her little brother Kenny hurry over. Lady Dill hops off her sofa to hurry over to give hugs. "I feel especially close to Corlett Caves' tiny ones," she squeaks to them. "Betsy, you look positively worn out!" Lady Dill hurries her mouse friend towards a comfortable spot to sit. "You sit here and rest a bit, Betsy."

"Bless you, and thank you, Dilly," Betsy says.

Everyone settles down on the three sofas, and Claire, the rabbit, makes tea and is looking for little cookies or cakes to hand out. The little mice, Chippy, and baby rabbits, Emma and Kenny, head off to explore the new toy room. Ella and Fielding sit off in a corner discussing some Patcher ideas. Lady Dill wonders, *Could I ever be happier than I feel right now?*

Lady Dill looks around her new home, seeing her friends. My new door comes later today or tomorrow, with Rob and Ernest and their wives already carving and shaping wood to be certain all will be secure.

Along to Lady Dill's home came the scrounger who had done the damage to Lady Dill's cave home.. Everyone suddenly becomes quiet, as the scrounger says short hellos and makes her way into the new home of Lady Dill.

"I hope I can come by, too," says the scrounger to Lady Dill. "I am sorry I took some of your items."

"Oh, thank you for coming by," Lady Dill says.

"My name is Pearl. I have had a tough time in life, but I am seeing it isn't your fault. I'm starting a group for scroungers, so we can talk about our issues." The scrounger looks about the room, and every animal stands quietly.

"Oh, okay. I'll spread the word." Lady Dill wonders if Pearl likes her free home. No word of thanks comes as Lady Dil stands quietly. Lady Dill guesses Pearl might bring it up if she felt the need to share. It all felt a bit awkward, but Lady Dill thought, *Life goes on.* "Look, Pearl, please have some food," Lady Dill says.

Pearl shook her head no and walks back up the tunnel, leaving the other animals. Lady Dill calls out a good-bye, but she also waves a paw to her friends, signaling them to not talk about Pearl. "Life goes on. Anyone can change," she reminds them.

Lady Dill stands from her resting spot and begins thanking everyone happily, jotting down the names of those rabbits who are going to be getting a warm carrot pie soon, as her way of thanking them. "Even though winter is coming, I will gather my winter foods, and I will gather straight sticks for my new fence. I will also dig up a few flower bulbs for my garden." Lady Dill has never been so full of plans and ideas. "Oh, and I must write myself a note to talk with Ann about the meal day ideas."

Benjamin bangs a spoon against a glass, and the whole room of animals grows quiet. All want to hear what the small gray mouse has to say. "Lady Dill, you've always been so willing to help us with anything we need. Looking around and seeing so many of us showing up today, well, that means we really want to help you because of your caring ways."

The room erupts with many cheers for Lady Dill. "My thanks to each of you," Lady Dill calls. She begins telling them about Fielding and Ella's idea of a working meals day by adds, "and each of us with extra harvest, let's bring it together to share with those who are less fortunate. Ms. Ann is here in case anyone didn't meet her, but I think she's heading home."

"I am heading down the ole country road," says Ann. "Bye, folks!" Ann heads up the tunnel and out of Lady Dill's new home.

Lady Dill sees Ann heading out, so she calls out to all, "My friend Ann says she's willing to help us with baking bread, and we can have some acorn nut soup warm and ready." Lady Dill hears cheers and farewells, as her guests head up and out of the tunnel to get to their homes before dusky darkness descends.

Full of hopeful activities on her horizon, Lady Dill happily settles into her new home, so filled with friends earlier and so full of hopeful plans now. Franklin and Trevor want to make a list of helpful chores. Ella wants to make some cloth napkins to use in the meals area. Every animal seems to have an idea to share.

"Winter, you can come soon, and I will be ready," Lady Dill calls out the door towards the entryway high above her. As her friends are heading up the tunnel, all thoughts are on the coming harvest to prepare for winter. Animals are heading up the tunnel, making the turns until they all reach the base of the live oak tree. Lady Dill follows them to give her last farewells. "Good-bye friends and mouselings! Good-bye, Miss Chips. Good-bye!" Lady Dill says, waving.

Once all becomes quiet, Lady Dill shuts her eyes again, leaning back to the beautiful tree, thinking, *pretty Tree, I promise to never harm you.* She pats the tree trunk, thinking, *thank you for my home down in the ground near your strong roots.* Faint twinkling lights from above her startle Lady Dill. She looks up to see that they seem to fill the thick, spreading branches of the live oak's branches. *I wonder what those sparkling lights are? How magical they seem,* she thinks. She heads to her tunnel's opening. Sparkles glisten throughout the tree's massive branches. *What a magical place*, she thinks as she hurries down into her new home.

The End

About the Author

 Sue Pumphrey collected acorns as a child, hiding them in her closet. At age five, she began writing letters to her two grandmothers. Sue grew up living in many states and two other countries, England and Japan, but now she lives in Huntsville, Alabama with her husband, a Pomeranian named Nugget, and two rescued cats, Ella and Jodie. Sue is a mom of five and a grandmother of three. Sue earned a Bachelor of Arts degree in English. She hopes her story shows the value of hard work, home, and helpfulness. She shows many generations of animals working together to face challenges. She wants her stories to include those with different disabilities including autism and physical disabilities, and she also hopes to highlight what conflicts loved ones feel when scroungers are nearby. She hopes her story will encourage young people to read but also give kids some quality in their books. She hopes to write more Corlett Caves books: for winter, spring, and summer. Sue hopes young people around the world can have good chapter books to read. She hopes readers will be sure to look for references to an Oscar-winning Robert Donat classic movie, set in a boys' school, *Good-bye, Mr. Chips* and to a Beatrix Potter character she loves from *The Tale of Johnny Townmouse.*